THE BABY-SITTERS CLUB®

BOY-CRAZY STACEY

**DON'T MISS THE OTHER
BABY-SITTERS CLUB GRAPHIC NOVELS!**

KRISTY'S GREAT IDEA

THE TRUTH ABOUT STACEY

MARY ANNE SAVES THE DAY

CLAUDIA AND MEAN JANINE

DAWN AND THE IMPOSSIBLE THREE

KRISTY'S BIG DAY

ANN M. MARTIN

THE BABY-SITTERS CLUB®

BOY-CRAZY STACEY

A GRAPHIC NOVEL BY

GALE GALLIGAN

WITH COLOR BY BRADEN LAMB

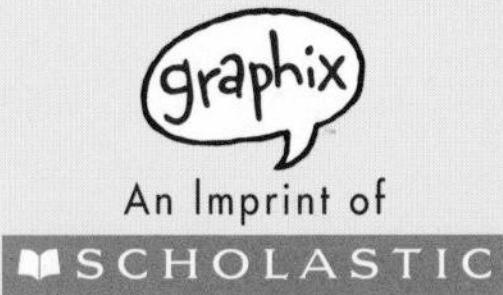

Library of Congress Control Number: 2018953576

ISBN 978-1-338-30452-7 (hardcover)
ISBN 978-1-338-30451-0 (paperback)

10 9 8 7 6 5 4 3 2 1   19 20 21 22 23

Printed in China   62
First edition, September 2019

Edited by Cassandra Pelham Fulton and David Levithan
Book design by Phil Falco
Publisher: David Saylor

This book is for June and Ward Cleaver
(alias Noël and Steve) from the Beav

A. M. M.

For Mom, Dad, Lori, and all
our childhood beach adventures.

And for Patrick, who I forgive for pretending to be
a sea monster and grabbing my ankle that one time.

G. G.

KRISTY THOMAS
PRESIDENT

CLAUDIA KISHI
VICE PRESIDENT

MARY ANNE SPIER
SECRETARY

STACEY MCGILL
TREASURER

DAWN SCHAFER
ALTERNATE OFFICER

MALLORY PIKE
JUNIOR OFFICER

CHAPTER 1

MY CHILD, THE HUMAN HURRICANE.
MOM? WHAT DO YOU WEAR TO A MANSION?
WHAT NOW?
WE'RE ALL GOING OVER TO KRISTY'S NEW PLACE TODAY, AND I WANT TO MAKE SURE I'M DOING IT RIGHT.
HAVEN'T YOU BEEN THERE BEFORE?
YEAH, BUT NOT FOR A REGULAR HANGOUT. I BET HER NEIGHBORS ARE REALLY FANCY.
KRISTY EVEN SAID THEY HAD TO TAKE LOUIE TO A GROOMER BEFORE THEY MOVED SO HE'D FIT IN WITH THE OTHER DOGS!!
SWEETIE, KRISTY'S STILL GOING TO BE KRISTY NO MATTER WHERE SHE LIVES. I DON'T THINK YOU SHOULD WORRY ABOUT IT TOO MUCH.
AND THIS IS A CUTE SHIRT.
HMM.

HI. I'M STACEY MCGILL.
I'M THIRTEEN YEARS OLD, AND I'M A FEW WEEKS AWAY FROM STARTING EIGHTH GRADE.
I MOVED HERE FROM NEW YORK CITY, I LOVE FASHION, AND...
AND WILL YOU BE--?
MOM, YOU KNOW I'M ALWAYS CAREFUL ABOUT WHAT I EAT.
I HAVE TYPE I DIABETES.
THAT MEANS THAT MY BODY DOESN'T MAKE ENOUGH INSULIN, WHICH IT NEEDS TO TURN SUGAR INTO ENERGY. HAVING TOO MUCH OR NOT ENOUGH SUGAR IN MY SYSTEM IS VERY DANGEROUS, SO I HAVE TO WATCH MY LEVELS...
AND GIVE MYSELF INSULIN SHOTS EVERY DAY.
This is my pancreas
It doesn't produce enough insulin, which means my body can't convert sugar into energy on its own.
I keep track of my blood sugar levels with a glucose meter
It takes just a drop of blood from my finger.
BUT IT'S REALLY NOT A BIG DEAL IF YOU MANAGE IT RIGHT, WHICH I DO.
I JUST WISH MY PARENTS UNDERSTOOD THAT!

honk
THAT'S MY RIDE!
GOTTA GO. LOVE YOU!
kiss
DO YOU HAVE YOUR TEST STRIPS? YOUR INSULIN PEN? YOUR --
YES, YES, YES!
NIGHT, DAD!
OH! DO YOU NEED PRETZEL STICKS?
I CAN PUT SOME IN A BAG FOR YOU!
I'm **FINE!** BYE! LOVE YOU!

DID YOU HEAR ABOUT LOUIE?

I HEARD THEY TRIMMED HIS FUR AND GAVE HIM A FANCY BANDANNA AND **EVERYTHING.**

I'M GOING TO BE OUTCLASSED BY A **DOG!**

GIRLS, GIRLS. EVEN IF SHE LIVES IN A MANSION NOW, I'M SURE KRISTY'S GOING TO BE THE SAME OLD...

WOW.

chips
KRISTYYY!!
HEY!!

AS I MENTIONED, I MOVED HERE FROM NEW YORK CITY LAST YEAR. I WAS WORRIED ABOUT MAKING NEW FRIENDS AT FIRST, BUT BEFORE I KNEW IT, I'D BECOME A MEMBER OF THE BABY-SITTERS CLUB.
CLAUDIA KISHI, VICE PRESIDENT. STYLE INSPIRATION, INCREDIBLE ARTIST, AND MY BEST FRIEND.
DAWN SCHAFER, ALTERNATE OFFICER. CALIFORNIAN, VEGETARIAN, VERY COOL.
AND ME! CLUB TREASURER.

KRISTY THOMAS, PRESIDENT. HER MOM JUST MARRIED A MILLIONAIRE, SO HERE WE ARE.
MARY ANNE SPIER, SECRETARY. A LITTLE SHY, BUT REALLY SMART AND THOUGHTFUL.
MALLORY PIKE, JUNIOR OFFICER AND NEWEST MEMBER. LOVES BOOKS AND BIG SWEATERS.
I CALL THIS MEETING OF THE BABY-SITTERS CLUB TO OR--
NO! THIS IS A **PARTY**!
poff

I CAN'T BELIEVE WE'RE ALL SPLITTING UP FOR TWO WEEKS!
YEAH, HAVE WE BEEN APART FOR THAT LONG SINCE THE CLUB STARTED?

UGH! ALL OF YOU ARE GOING TO HAVE SO MUCH **FUN.** AND HERE I'LL BE, ENJOYING **NEW FAMILY BONDING TIME.**

DAWN'S GOING TO VISIT HER DAD IN CALIFORNIA...
GUILTY.

CLAUDIA AND HER FAMILY WILL BE LOUNGING AROUND AT A RESORT IN NEW HAMPSHIRE...
THE FRESH AIR SHOULD BE REALLY GOOD FOR MIMI.

AND MARY ANNE AND STACEY...
GET TO BABY-SIT THE PIKES ON THEIR **ANNUAL BEACH VACATION!!**
hee hee

THERE ARE EIGHT PIKE KIDS INCLUDING MALLORY. SHE HAS IT TOUGH SOMETIMES, BECAUSE SHE'S THE OLDEST AND ENDS UP TAKING CARE OF THEM A LOT.
MR. AND MRS. PIKE THOUGHT IT'D BE NICE TO HIRE ME AND MARY ANNE TO BABY-SIT, SO MALLORY COULD REALLY ENJOY HERSELF THIS YEAR.
Junior Officer!
Triplets!!!
Mallory (11)
Claire (5)
Margo (7)
Vanessa (9)
Byron (10)
Jordan (10)
Adam (10)
Nicky (8)
I HAD TO ADMIT THAT I WAS A LITTLE NERVOUS. MARY ANNE AND I WERE FRIENDS, BUT WE WEREN'T AS CLOSE AS, SAY, ME AND CLAUDIA.
AND WE'RE **SO** DIFFERENT FROM EACH OTHER!
• outgoing
• sophisticated
• romantic
• shy
• sensitive
• thoughtful
Not to mention our fashion sense!
THAT SAID...THERE WAS NO WAY MARY ANNE OR I COULD SAY NO TO A **PAID BEACH TRIP!**
OH MY GOSH, IT'S ALMOST TIME FOR OUR PARENTS TO PICK US UP.
I WON'T SEE YOU GUYS FOR **TWO WEEKS!!**
HEY, I HAVE AN IDEA.

LET'S EXCHANGE OUR VACATION ADDRESSES. THEN WE CAN ALL WRITE EACH OTHER POSTCARDS!
THAT'S A GOOD IDEA.
IF WE WRITE ABOUT OUR BABY-SITTING JOBS, WE CAN COPY THEM INTO THE NOTEBOOK LATER, TOO.
DAWN? MARY ANNE? YOUR PARENTS ARE HERE.
TWO WEEKS!!
I'M GOING TO MISS YOU!
I'M GOING TO MISS YOU AND BE BOOORED!!

IT HURT TO IMAGINE BEING AWAY FOR SO LONG...

BUT I COULDN'T HELP GETTING EXCITED ABOUT THE SUN...THE SURF...

CHAPTER 2

BRACE YOURSELF.
ding dong
tPtPtPtPdada
CRASH
HIIIII!
MARY ANNE! STACEY!!
COME IN!
COME IN!!
grab!

TOMORROW, TOMORROW, WE GO TO SEA CITY!
WE'LL SEE THE BEACH AND THE SHELLS SO PRETTY!
SHE THINKS SHE'S A POET.
I AM SO A POET! AND YOU SHOULD KNOW IT!
POETS DON'T HAVE TO RHYME EVERYTHING!!
RHYMING'S AN ART, YOU STINKY --
KIDS, KIDS!
MARY ANNE AND STACEY AND I HAVE TO TALK BUSINESS. GIVE US A MOMENT, OKAY?
SORRY ABOUT THAT.
NO, NO. THANK YOU FOR HAVING US.

I ASKED YOU OVER HERE TODAY SO WE COULD TALK ABOUT WHAT YOU'LL BE DOING IN SEA CITY, AND SET SOME GROUND RULES.
MOSTLY, YOU'LL JUST BE GIVING MR. PIKE AND ME A HAND SINCE, OF COURSE, WE'LL BE THERE, TOO.
BUT WE WOULD LIKE A LITTLE TIME TO OURSELVES AS WELL.

THERE WILL BE AFTERNOONS OR EVENINGS WHEN WE'LL GO OFF TO DO THINGS ON OUR OWN. THAT'S WHEN YOU'LL BE IN CHARGE.
THERE'S A LOT TO SEE AND DO IN SEA CITY, AND YOU SHOULD BE PERFECTLY SAFE ON YOUR OWN. JUST KEEP A CAREFUL EYE ON THE CHILDREN WHEN YOU'RE CROSSING THE STREET.

nod

AND WE HAVE ONE BEACH RULE.

ABSOLUTELY NO GOING IN THE OCEAN, NOT EVEN WADING, BEFORE NINE A.M. OR AFTER FIVE P.M. THAT'S WHEN THE LIFEGUARDS ARE OFF DUTY.
ASIDE FROM THAT, THE KIDS CAN SWIM AS MUCH AS THEY WANT AS LONG AS THEY STAY IN FRONT OF THE LIFEGUARD STATION. OKAY?
OKAY.

AFTER THAT, MRS. PIKE TOLD US A LITTLE MORE ABOUT SEA CITY AND THE HOUSE THEY'D RENTED THERE, AS WELL AS THINGS LIKE GROCERY SHOPPING AND DIVIDING UP CHORES.
I ALSO REMINDED HER OF MY DIET AND HOW I WOULD BE MANAGING MY DIABETES.
ALL RIGHT! I'LL SEE YOU BRIGHT AND EARLY TOMORROW.
EIGHT O'CLOCK!

AND WITH THAT, IT WAS TIME TO GO HOME AND PACK.
stacey's two-
cute tops
SUNSCREEN!
no BURN
SPF 60
(don't forget!!)
toiletry bag
NY
bikini!!
strappy heels

week beach bag
sundresses
a good book
sweater
(just in case)
diabetes travel kit
embroidery
shorts & jeans
flip-flops

STACEY? YOU ALL PACKED?
JUST FINISHED!
zip

AND YOU'RE SET FOR TWO WEEKS?
YUP.

YOU HAVE TOOTHPASTE?
YUP.
STAMPS FOR POSTCARDS?
YUP.
AND...

sigh
MOM, I'VE GOT MY DIABETES KIT RIGHT HERE.

THE DOCTORS' NUMBERS ARE IN MY PURSE, AND THE PIKES HAVE A COPY, TOO.
I ALSO TOLD MRS. PIKE ALL ABOUT MY DIET TODAY.
THERE'S NOTHING TO WORRY ABOUT.
OH, STACEY.
I'M GOING TO WORRY MYSELF SICK.
MOM, IT'S OKAY. THE PIKES HAVE A PHONE. THEY'LL CALL IF ANYTHING HAPPENS. AND... YOU CAN CALL IF YOU GET WORRIED.
ALTHOUGH MAYBE DON'T CALL TOO OFTEN.

THE PIKE KIDS WON'T LISTEN TO ME IF THEY THINK I HAVE TO CHECK IN WITH MY MOM FOR EVERYTHING.

IT SURE IS HARD HELPING YOUR PARENTS WATCH YOU GROW UP.

BUT IT HAS TO BE DONE.

SEA CITY
NJ
"Greetings from Paradise!"

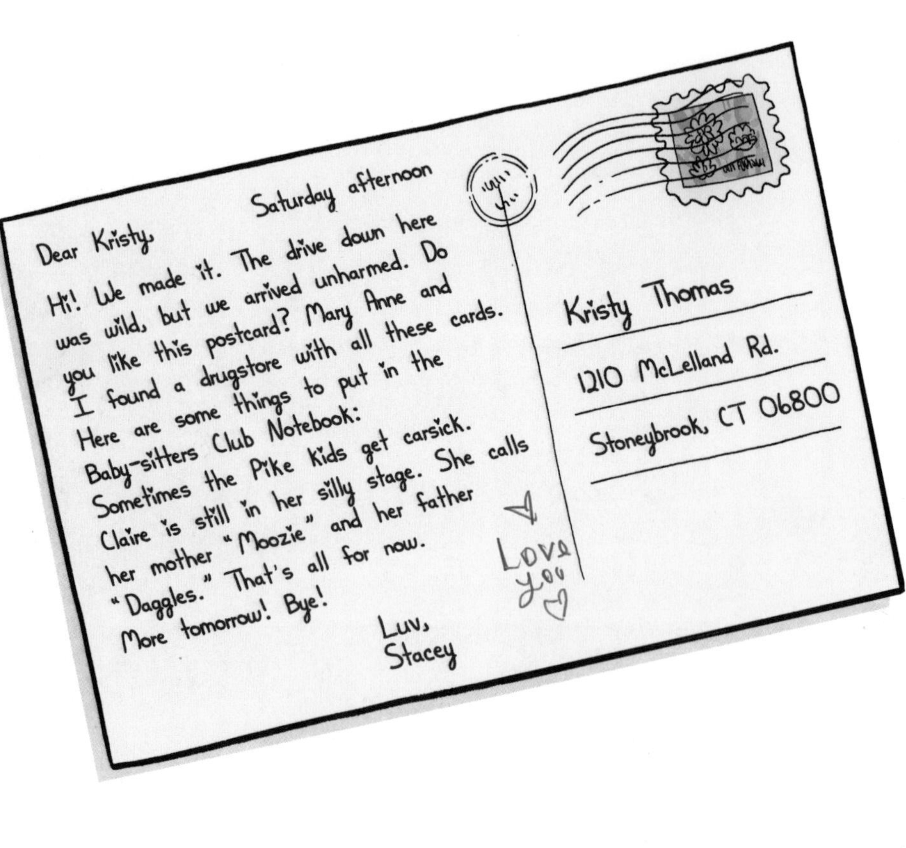
Saturday afternoon
Dear Kristy,
Hi! We made it. The drive down here
was wild, but we arrived unharmed. Do
you like this postcard? Mary Anne and
I found a drugstore with all these cards.
Here are some things to put in the
Baby-sitters Club Notebook:
Sometimes the Pike kids get carsick.
Claire is still in her silly stage. She calls
her mother "Moozie" and her father
"Daggles." That's all for now.
More tomorrow! Bye!
Luv,
Stacey
Love you
Kristy Thomas
1210 McLelland Rd.
Stoneybrook, CT 06800

CHAPTER 3

YOU DOUBLE-CHECKED THE TEST STRIPS? AND YOUR GLUCOSE METER?
DOUBLE AND TRIPLE.

HI, STACEY! GOOD MORNING, MR. MCGILL!

WELL, LOOKS LIKE I'M NOT THE ONLY DAD WHO'LL MISS HIS DAUGHTER.

HI, STACEY-SILLY-BILLY-GOO-GOO!
MARY ANNE-SILLY-BILLY-GOO-GOO!!

WHEW. I THINK THAT'S --

thunk

WHAT'S THIS?
BEDDING.
TOYS.

UUUUUUUGHHHHH.

FORTY-FIVE MINUTES LATER, EVERYTHING WAS FINALLY PACKED AND READY TO GO.
ALL RIGHT, TEAM, HERE'S THE PLAN.
MARY ANNE, YOU'LL BE HELPING OUT IN MRS. PIKE'S CAR. STACEY, YOU'RE WITH ME.
WE'RE GOING TO MEET FOR A QUICK BREAK AT THE HALFWAY POINT, WHICH JUST SO HAPPENS TO BE HAPPY'S ICE CREAM.
ROGER.
AND WE WERE OFF!
PIKEMOBILE (#1)
Mr. Pike
Mallory
Nicky
me!
barf bucket
Margo
Claire
entertainment!
WAIT...
BARF BUCKET?

GOOD-BYE, HOUSE-SILLY-BILLY-GOO-GOO!!
SEA CITY, HERE WE COME!

HOW MUCH LONGER?
HOO BOY.

A FEW HOURS. WHY DON'T YOU AND MARGO TAKE OUT YOUR COLORING BOOKS?

YOU COULD DO A PAGE TO GIVE TO YOUR MOM.

EVERYTHING WAS QUIET FOR ABOUT AN HOUR, AND THEN...
HEY!
BARFMOBILE?!
BARF-MOBILE
DAD, SPEED UP, SPEED UP! WE HAVE TO CATCH THEM!
I DON'T FEEL SO GOOD...!!
AHHHHHH!!!

Happy's Ice Cream
Enter
SILLY-BILLY!!
ICE CREAM! ICE CREEEAM!!
WHEEEW.
HOW'S YOUR RIDE BEEN?
EVERYTHING WAS FINE...UNTIL THE BARFMOBILE SIGN.
haha
SORRY ABOUT THAT.
JUST A FEW HOURS TO GO!

NICKY, FOR THE LAST TIME, QUIT IT!
QUIT WHAT? I'M NOT DOING ANYTHING.
I CAN **HEAR** YOU. YOU'RE WHISPERING ABOUT ME.
MUST BE YOUR IMAGINATION. I'M JUST SITTING HERE QUIETLY, SAYING NOTHING AT ALL ABOUT YOUR FACE.
KNOCK IT OFF, YOU TWO.
BUT I DIDN'T **DO** ANYTHING!
YOU'RE MAKING A RACKET!
HEY, EVERYBODY! LOOK!!

Welcome to
SEA CITY
NEW JERSEY

hello!
BEST
DOGS

Saturday night

Dear Claudia,

Hi! We've been in Sea City for half a day now. You should have seen the kids today after we got here. We went exploring as soon as we were unpacked, and they were so excited! There's so much to do here!

After we looked around the town, we took a walk on the beach. I saw the most gorgeous boy! He's a lifeguard, and he's the guy of my dreams!

See ya!

Luv,
Stace

Claudia Kishi
Sky Mountain Resort
Lincoln, NH 03251

FOREVER USA

SEA CITY, NJ

CHAPTER 4

The Perfect Cast
SO YOU GUYS COME TO THIS SAME HOUSE EVERY YEAR?
YEAH, WE'VE BEEN REALLY LUCKY. IT'S RIGHT ON THE BEACH AND EVERYTHING.
SOMETIMES IN THE EVENING WE JUST SIT ON THE PORCH AND WATCH THE OCEAN.
AND WHEN IT RAINS...
THERE'S THIS ROOM ON THE THIRD FLOOR WITH A WINDOW SEAT WHERE YOU CAN CURL UP AND ENJOY THE LIGHTNING AND CRASHING WAVES.

SAME ROOMS AS LAST YEAR! BOYS IN THE BIG BEDROOM AT THE END OF THE HALL.
CLAIRE AND MARGO, YOU'RE NEXT TO DADDY AND ME. VANESSA AND MALLORY, THE PINK ROOM.
MALLORY, SHOW STACEY AND MARY ANNE THE YELLOW ROOM, OKAY?
WOW.
THIS IS GONNA BE GREAT!!

SO, WHAT DO YOU ALL WANT TO DO THIS AFTERNOON?
GO TO THE BEACH.
I WANNA MAKE SANDCASTLES.
THE FERRIS WHEEL!
THE ARCADE!
WE COULD GO TO TRAMPOLINE LAND.

WELL...MAYBE WE CAN DO EVERYTHING... SORT OF.
SORT OF?
STACEY AND I HAVEN'T BEEN HERE BEFORE. WHY DON'T YOU ALL TAKE US ON A TOUR?
WE MIGHT NOT HAVE TIME TO **DO** ALL THE THINGS, BUT WE CAN AT LEAST SEE THE TOWN.
YEAH!!
EVERYONE FINISHED EATING PRETTY QUICKLY AFTER THAT, AND THEN WE WERE OFF TO SEE SEA CITY!
SEA CITY SURF

I ♥ Sea City
I ♥ Sea City

A FEW HOURS LATER, WE FOUND OURSELVES BACK AT THE BEACH IN FRONT OF THE PIKES' HOUSE.
HMM, LOOKS LIKE THE LIFEGUARDS ARE PACKING UP.
I DON'T THINK YOU SHOULD GET IN THE WATER, BUT YOU CAN PLAY ON THE BEACH.
I'M GONNA GO GET THE PADDLEBALL STUFF FROM THE HOUSE!
YEAH!!
AHHHHH.
YOU SAID IT.

POSTCARD

Dear Kristy,

Sunday

Here's something for the notebook: Pikes get up early. See ya!

Stacey

Kristy Thomas
1210 McLelland Rd.
Stoneybrook, CT 06800

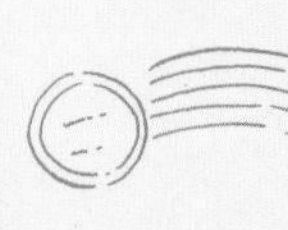

Sunday

Dear Claudia,

Today I found out that gooorgeous lifeguard's name. It's SCOTT!! I can't wait to see him again.

Luv,
Stace

P.S. I can't let Mary Anne see this card. She doesn't understand about Scott at all. She thinks I've lost it.

Claudia Kishi
Sky Mountain Resort
Lincoln, NH 03251

CHAPTER 5

STACEY?
STACEY?
STACEY, LET'S GO TO THE BEACH.
WE WANNA GO TO THE BEEEEEACH.

5:24 A
STACEY...? WHAT'S...?
THESE TWO WANT TO HIT THE BEACH, AND IT'S BARELY EVEN MORNING.
STACEEEEY. IT'S OUR FIRST DAY AT THE BEEEEACH AND THE SUN IS UUUUP.
STACEEEEEEEEY.
TOO EARLY. SLEEP NOW.

BACON.

THE KIDS ALL SCARFED DOWN BREAKFAST...

AND THEN IT WAS OFF TO THE RACES.

HMM.

DO YOU THINK SOMETHING'S UP WITH BYRON?
WHAT DO YOU MEAN?

BYRON! COME ON!
NO, THANKS.

YOU'RE SO BORING!
LAAAME!

HE KNOWS HOW TO SWIM, DOESN'T HE?
YEAH, THE KIDS WERE ALL TAKING LESSONS LAST YEAR.
I WONDER IF --

OHHHHMIGOSH.
IT'S HIM.
HUH?
THE BEAUTIFUL LIFEGUARD.
HE SMILED AT ME YESTERDAY. HIS HAIR...HIS EYES... MARY ANNE, I'M IN LOVE.
UM.

AND THE MOMENT OUR EYES MET... IT WAS LIKE, WOW.
I KNOW, I KNOW. HE'S CUTE AND HE'S A LIFEGUARD, DON'T GET MY HOPES UP.
BUT HE LOOKED RIGHT AT ME AND SMILED! YOU SAW IT, RIGHT, MARY ANNE?
GOSH, I WONDER IF I SHOULD JUST GO OVER AND SAY HI.
SHOULD I? WOULD THAT BE WEIRD?
SCAREDY-CAT!
BABY!!
QUIT IT!
Splash splash
HEY. WHAT'S ALL THIS ABOUT?
HE WON'T COME IN THE WATER!!
US TRIPLETS ARE SUPPOSED TO STICK TOGETHER AND HE'S RUINING IT!

WHO DECIDED THAT YOU TRIPLETS **HAD** TO GO INTO THE WATER?

WHAT ABOUT WHAT BYRON WANTS TO DO?

WELL...I MEAN... IT'S THE **BEACH!**

AND IS THE BEACH MADE O JUST WAT

+LIFEGUARD+
HEY THERE.
H-HEY.
I -- um --
AAAAAAGH!!

WHAT HAPPENED?
SHE CUT HER FOOT ON A SHELL.
aaaaaaaaa
ALLOW ME.
LIFEGUARD+LIFEGUARD+
GUARD+LIF
I'M SCOTT, BY THE WAY.
SCOTT. I'M STACEY.
EGUARD+LIFEG
UARD+LIFEG

FOR THE REST OF THE DAY, I KEPT FINDING EXCUSES TO GO BACK AND TALK TO SCOTT.
Scott Foley
EVERYTHING I FOUND OUT ABOUT HIM JUST MADE ME LIKE HIM MORE.
15 years old!
from Princeton, NJ!
LIFEGUARD + LIFEGUARD + LI
HE'D GROWN UP NEAR NEW YORK CITY, HE WAS IMPRESSED WHEN I TOLD HIM I WAS A BABY-SITTER...
& likes cats!!!
I WAS ABSOLUTELY, COMPLETELY, ONE HUNDRED PERCENT IN L-O-V-
STACEY.
+LIFEG

ARE YOU EVEN LISTENING? I UNDERSTAND THAT THE LIFEGUARD IS CUTE, BUT WE'RE STILL HERE TO DO A JOB.

YOU'VE BEEN LEAVING ME ALONE WITH THE KIDS A LOT TODAY, AND IT'S REALLY FRUSTRATING.

STACEY?

SCOTT.

IT LOOKED LIKE ADAM WAS GOING TO SPIKE THE BALL RIGHT AT ME, BUT THEN --
I BACKED INTO THIS BIG THING OF SEAWEED!
I'M GOING FOR A QUICK WALK.
Stacey
+
SC
Scott

workin' like a DOG!

Dear Kristy,

Monday

A problem with Nicky. The triplets think he's babyish, so they don't play with him. But there are no other boys in the family, and he doesn't like getting stuck with the girls, especially Vanessa.

I feel kinda sorry for him.

Luv,
Stacey

Kristy Thomas
1210 McLelland Rd.
Stoneybrook, CT 06800

Dear Dawn,

Monday

Hi! How is sunny California? Guess what? I am sunburned. I look like a tomato with hair.

Love,
Mary Anne

Dawn Schafer
88 Palm Blvd.
Palo City, CA 92800

CHAPTER 6

SCOTT WAS OFF DUTY THE NEXT DAY, BUT I COULDN'T STOP THINKING ABOUT HIM.

HE SEEMED HAPPY WHENEVER I CAME BY TO TALK TO HIM. DID THAT MEAN HE LIKED ME?

OR WAS I TOO OBVIOUS? WHAT IF SCOTT THOUGHT I WAS TRYING TOO HARD??

THE WHOLE DAY WENT BY IN A HAZE, BUT THEN...

I'D LIKE TO TAKE MR. PIKE TO DINNER TONIGHT. WOULD YOU BE ALL RIGHT WATCHING THE KIDS FOR THE EVENING?
WE WERE THINKING YOU COULD TAKE THEM TO --
BURGER GARDEN!!
GURBER GARDEN!
THE WAITERS ALL DRESS LIKE ANIMALS AND THERE'S A BIG, BIG TREE AND --
WHAT A FUN AND TASTY WAY TO END THIS BRIGHT AND SUNNY DAY!
WE SIT ON MUSHROOMS TO EAT!
YOU HAVE TO GET A CRAZY BURGER! THEY HAVE ORANGE SAUCE!!
LAST YEAR I WON A COLORING CONTEST AND GOT TWO CRAZY BURGERS AND A FANTASY FOUNTAIN SODA AND --
THE ORANGE SAUCE IS BECAUSE THEY MIX KETCHUP AND MUSTARD TOGETHER AND IT'S THE BEST!!
MUSHROOM! MUSHROOM!!

WHOA.

WELCOME TO BURGER GARDEN! FOLLOW ME!

WELL, THIS IS ANOTHER FIRST.

MY FIRST TRIP AWAY FROM HOME, MY FIRST TIME AT THE JERSEY SHORE...
MY FIRST TIME BEING SERVED BY AN ANIMAL...

YOUR FIRST TIME EATING ON A MUSHROOM.
IT REALLY IS A MAGICAL SUMMER.

GO SIT WITH VANESSA.
NO, I WANT TO SIT WITH YOU GUYS.
US TRIPLETS ARE SITTING ALONE.
NO, YOU'RE NOT, BECAUSE I'M SITTING WITH YOU.
WHERE WILL I SIT?
SIT WITH US, NICKY-SILLY-BILLY-GOO-GOO!
WHAT'S THE MATTER, WHAT'S THE FUSS? SIT WITH ME, I'LL --
NO!!

IN THE END, NICKY AGREED TO SIT WITH VANESSA ON THE CONDITION THAT SHE FLIP OFF HER POETRY SWITCH FOR THE NIGHT, AND I LEFT THE TRIPLETS ALONE.
THE KIDS WERE GOOD, FOR THE MOST PART...
SO AFTER DINNER, WE LET THEM EACH BUY A MYSTERY EGG FROM THE ENCHANTED TREE.
LUCKY!
NICE!!
TURNS OUT THAT IF YOU HAVE A COUPON FOR FOUR FREE DINNERS AT BURGER GARDEN, THE TRIPLETS WILL BE YOUR VERY BEST FRIENDS.

AFTER THAT, WE GAVE EACH KID A FEW DOLLARS AND TOOK SOME TIME TO ENJOY THE BOARDWALK.
HAUNT
HOUS
SURES

ONE HOUR LATER, WE ALL MET BACK UP AT ICE CREAM PALACE.
ACE
CREAM

OKAY. I'M NOT GOING TO HAVE ANY ICE CREAM, SO THAT MEANS THERE'S ENOUGH FOR ONE SCOOP FOR EACH OF YOU.
AND SPRINKLES.

I'M NOT GOING TO HAVE ANY, EITHER, SO THERE'S A LITTLE EXTRA.
OH. WAIT, ARE YOU FEELING OKAY? YOU LOOK KIND OF FUNNY.

I DON'T KNOW. I FEEL HOT ON THE OUTSIDE, BUT...CHILLY?
OH MY GOSH.

YOU'RE SUNBURNED!!
NOOOOOOOOO.

WE GOT MARY ANNE SOME ICE CREAM TO COOL HER DOWN...

AND THEN OUR SECOND BEACH DAY CAME TO A CLOSE.

WHAT DID I DO TO DESERVE THISSSSSS.

MARY ANNE?

I BROUGHT MOISTURIZER.

A BOTTLE OF WATER.

COLD COMPRESSES.

MOM'S ALOE CREAM.

A LITTLE FAN. IT LIGHTS UP.

TEA BAGS FOR YOUR EYELIDS.

AND I BROUGHT PEANUT BUTTER.

aloe

ha
ha

Dear Claudia,

Tuesday

I know I'm supposed to be baby-sitting, but Scott was on duty today and he's all I can think of. He said the sweetest thing when I went to say good-bye for the day . . . I can't wait to tell you all about it. Say hi to Mimi!

Luv,
Stace

P.S. Mary Anne thinks I'm overthinking it. She doesn't understand.

Claudia Kishi
Sky Mountain Resort
Lincoln, NH 03251

Tuesday

Dear Kristy,

I'd never have suspected it, but Byron has a lot of fears. He's afraid to go in the ocean (even though he can swim), and last night when we went to the amusement park on the boardwalk, he wouldn't go through the haunted house. We'll have to talk about this.

Luv,
Stacey

Kristy Thomas
1210 McLelland Rd.
Stoneybrook, CT 06800

CHAPTER 7
I'M SORRY, MARY ANNE.
I'M A TOMATOOOOOOO.
A BEAUTIFUL, SMART TOMATO.

mermaid
PHWEEEET!
LIFEGUARD

HEY, GUYS.
HEY, SCOTT.
STACE! YOU'RE HERE!

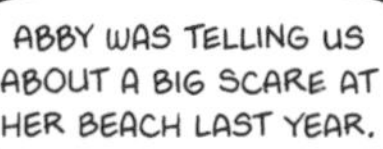
ABBY WAS TELLING US ABOUT A BIG SCARE AT HER BEACH LAST YEAR.

OH? WHAT HAPPENED?

THIS KID THOUGHT HE'D BEEN STUNG BY A JELLYFISH...
BUT HIS SISTER HAD JUST PINCHED HIM UNDERWATER.
hahahaha

THAT REMINDS ME OF THE TIME...

HEY, UH, NEED SOME COMPANY?
MY NAME'S ALEX.

I NOTICED YOU WERE WATCHING KIDS, TOO.
I'M WITH MY LITTLE COUSINS OVER THERE.
KENNY, ELLIE, AND JIMMY. THEY CAN BE A BIT OF A HANDFUL, BUT THEY'RE CUTE.
YEAH, I'M BABY-SITTING FOR MY FRIEND'S FAMILY. I'D BE OUT ON THE BEACH, BUT... SUNBURN.
OH NO! ARE YOU --
I SAID STOP!
JEEZ! IT WAS JUST A LITTLE WATER!
SORRY. THE TRIPLETS HAVE BEEN GETTING IN FIGHTS ALL WEEK.
TRIPLE TROUBLE.
BUT WAIT. THERE'S ANOTHER BABY-SITTER HERE WITH YOU, RIGHT? SHOULDN'T SHE BE HELPING OUT?
GOOD QUESTION.

SHARK!!

EVERYBODY OUT!
GET OUT OF THE WATER!
MARY ANNE!!
I'VE GOT CLAIRE AND ADAM!
WE'RE HERE!

WHERE'S THE SHARK? WHERE'S THE SHARK??
I-IS THAT IT THERE?
OHHHH.
WOW.
PHWEET!
FALSE ALARM!
LOOKS LIKE A GARBAGE BAG.

FOR THE REST OF THE DAY, I ALTERNATED BETWEEN TRYING TO CONVINCE BYRON THAT THE WATER WAS SAFE...

AND FINDING REASONS TO GO OVER AND TALK TO SCOTT.

THE MORE WE GOT TO KNOW EACH OTHER, THE HARDER I FELL.
HE WAS KIND, FUNNY, CHARMING... AND SO CUTE!

I JUST HAD ONE LITTLE PROBLEM.

WHENEVER I GLANCED BACK AT MARY ANNE, SHE WAS GLARING DAGGERS AT ME.

BUT I COULD SEE THE KIDS JUST FINE FROM THE LIFEGUARD STAND!
AND ANYWAY, THAT OTHER BOY WAS OVER THERE HELPING HER ALL THE TIME!!

I THINK WE SHOULD TAKE THEM INSIDE. JORDAN LOOKS KIND OF BURNED, AND CLAIRE'S JUST BURNING OUT.
OKAY, YOU START. I NEED TO --
STACEY. I CAN'T DO THIS ALL BY MYSELF. THERE'S SO MUCH TO PACK UP, AND THE KIDS TO WATCH.
YOU HAVE EIGHT KIDS TO HELP YOU! AND THAT OTHER BOY WHO KEEPS SHOWING UP!
BUT WE'RE THE ONES GETTING PAID TO --
I'LL BE BACK IN ONE MINUTE! THANKS, MARY ANNE!!

SCOTT!
OH! HEY, STACE!

JUST A SEC, DAVE. I'LL BE RIGHT THERE.

I JUST WANTED TO SAY...

THANKS FOR COMING BY THE LAST FEW DAYS.
YOU'RE REALLY FUN.

HONK!

AT THAT MOMENT...

I KNEW...I JUST KNEW.

SCOTT WAS IN LOVE
WITH ME, TOO!!

MARTY'S
Mini Golf

Dear Kristy,

Thursday

Today the weather was awful. Stacey and I must have been out of our minds: we took the kids to the miniature golf course. But guess what? We had a great time. Sometimes I think that eight kids aren't any harder to take care of than two or three. The Pikes argue and tease, but they also help each other out.

Love,
Mary Anne

Kristy Thomas
1210 McLelland Rd.
Stoneybrook, CT 06800

P.S. Stacey is being a real pain. She really is.

P.P.S. Don't ever show this card to her.

CHAPTER 8

YOU KNOW...
I THINK TODAY WOULD BE A GOOD DAY TO GO TO SMITHTOWN.
NOOOO.
DAD, PLEASE. NOT SMITHTOWN AGAIN.
WHAT'S SMITHTOWN?
IT'S A HOKEY OLD TOWN THAT'S SUPPOSED TO LOOK LIKE THE SEVENTEEN HUNDREDS OR SOMETHING.
I **ALWAYS** WEAR A FROWN WHEN I GO TO **SMITHTOWN.**

SMITHTOWN IS A VERY NICE RESTORED COLONIAL VILLAGE.
THERE ARE STORES AND HOUSES, A CHURCH, A BLACKSMITH, CRAFTSPEOPLE...
OOOOH.
BUUUT YOU KIDS DON'T HAVE TO GO IF YOU DON'T WANT TO.
whew
ARE YOU AND DAD GOING ANYWAY?
Hmm.
WHY NOT?
CAN YOU ALL FIND SOMETHING TO DO TODAY?
LEAVE IT TO US.
SO MR. AND MRS. PIKE HANDED ME AND MARY ANNE SOME MONEY, AND THEN THEY DROVE AWAY TO COLONIAL SMITHTOWN.
WE'D JUST HAVE TO FIND SOMETHING EVERYONE WANTED TO DO.

LOOKS LIKE WE HAVE SORRY, MONOPOLY, SOME JIGSAW PUZZLES...
WE DO THE PUZZLES EVERY YEAR, BUT THERE'S ALWAYS A PIECE MISSING.
AND CLAIRE CHEATS AT MONOPOLY.
OKAY, THEN. COLORING.
BOOOOORING.
SIBLINGS, SIBLINGS, DON'T BE BLUE! I, VANESSA, SHALL ENTERTAIN YOU!
GATHER ROUND, MAKE NO SOUND, AS THE POET WITH EYES OF --
NO!!!
YOU KNOW, IT'S NOT ACTUALLY RAINING ANYMORE.
WE COULD PROBABLY GO TO THE BOARDWALK, AT LEAST.

ONCE WE'D MADE IT TO
THE BOARDWALK, EVERYONE'S
DECISION WAS UNANIMOUS...
TODAY WAS A
GOOD DAY FOR
MINI GOLF.
I'M FIRST!
I'M FIRST!
whoosh

MAYBE WE SHOULD SPLIT INTO A FEW SEPARATE GROUPS.
GOOD IDEA.

ALL RIGHT! NOW THAT WE'VE MADE IT THROUGH, THERE'S JUST ONE THING LEFT TO DO.

SEND OUR BALLS UP INTO THAT CHUTE.
OKAY!!

thunk

tap

DING
DING
DING

SOMEBODY JUST WON TWO FREE GAMES!!
OH! OH, IT'S ME!!

CAN WE PLAY AGAIN NOW??

WHY DON'T WE SAVE THAT FOR THE NEXT RAINY DAY?
OKAY, STACEY-SILLY-BILLY-GOO-GOO.

hello from...
MY SUMMER HOME

Sun.

K-

Noth. new to rept. Kids fine. B. still afrd. of H_2O.

-S.

Kristy Thomas
1210 McLelland Rd.
Stoneybrook, CT 06800

Sunday

Dear Claudia,

The most awful, humiliating thing in the world has happened. I can't believe it. I feel like such a jerk. Mary Anne tried to warn me about Scott but I wouldn't listen. She told me not to fall too fast. She told me this, she told me that. And I wouldn't listen. Oh, I am such a jerk. (I guess I've run out of room. I'll tell you the rest in the next postcard.)

Luv,
Stace

Claudia Kishi
Sky Mountain Resort
Lincoln, NH 03251

CHAPTER 9

WE'D BEEN IN SEA CITY FOR JUST OVER A WEEK, AND THINGS WERE GOING SWIMMINGLY.

FRANKLY, I THINK SHE WAS JEALOUS. THAT OTHER BABY-SITTER KEPT HANGING AROUND HER WHENEVER HE HAD THE CHANCE, HELPING HER WITH THE KIDS AND MAKING SANDCASTLES AND STUFF...
AND, LET'S BE HONEST, HE WAS NOWHERE NEAR SCOTT'S LEAGUE.

BUT AS FOR HER COMPLAINTS! "STACEY, YOU'RE SPENDING TOO MUCH TIME WITH SCOTT! STACEY, YOU'RE SUPPOSED TO BE LOOKING AFTER THE CHILDREN!"

I WAS AT THE LIFEGUARD STAND, FOR HEAVEN'S SAKE. I HAD THE BEST VIEW OF THE KIDS, AND HALF OF THEM WERE IN THE WATER NONSTOP.

bonk
SO WASN'T **I** THE ONE WHO WAS ACTUALLY WATCHING THE KIDS MORE THAN MARY ANNE?

WOW, STACEY.
YOU'RE THE REAL DEAL.
LIFEGUARD

THAT AFTERNOON, MR. AND MRS. PIKE CAME BACK FROM ATLANTIC CITY IN A VERY GOOD MOOD...
AND GAVE ME AND MARY ANNE A BIT OF A SURPRISE.
HOW WOULD YOU TWO LIKE THE REST OF THE DAY OFF?
COME ON, MARY ANNE! PLEASE DON'T BE MAD AT ME.
WE HAVE FIVE WHOLE HOURS TO OURSELVES.
WE CAN GO TO THE BOARDWALK, HAVE A QUIET DINNER...
ENJOY THE RIDES, DO SOME SHOPPING...
FINE.
THAT SOUNDS GOOD.

FLOATS 'N' TOTES
MYSTERY MAZE
I'M REALLY GLAD WE CAME.

THIS PAST YEAR, I FEEL LIKE I'VE FINALLY STARTED...BECOMING MYSELF, IF THAT MAKES SENSE.

FIGURING OUT HOW **I** LIKE TO DRESS, STANDING UP FOR MYSELF, BEING MORE INDEPENDENT FROM DAD. COMING HERE FEELS LIKE ANOTHER STEP TOWARD THAT.
MARY ANNE, THAT'S REALLY COOL.

I KIND OF KNOW HOW YOU FEEL. MY PARENTS ARE GREAT, BUT...
THEY WORRY ABOUT ME A LOT.
YEAH.

I SHOULD BUY SCOTT A PRESENT.
AGH.

EVERYBODY LIKES HATS, RIGHT?
EH.

SOMETHING FOR HIM TO THINK ABOUT ON THE BEACH.
I DUNNO...

OOH, MARY ANNE! THEY'RE CONNECTED BY A LITTLE HEART!
UGH.

I COULD --
NO. NOPE. DEFINITELY NOT.
SEA CITY
Tobias Rachel
While U Wait

DO YOU THINK HE'LL LIKE IT?
UM...MAYBE. DOES HE LIKE CHOCOLATE?
PROBABLY. NO MATTER WHAT, THIS SHOULD REALLY SHOW HIM HOW I FEEL.
DON'T YOU THINK?
...MARY ANNE?
STACEY --
WAIT, DON'T --

STACEY --
C-CONGRATULATIONS. YOU WERE **RIGHT.**
I WON'T BE NEEDING TH-THIS --

ANYM--
sob

sob sob sob

snf
C'MON, STACE.
LET'S GO.

Dear Dawn,

Sunday night

Stacey is still being a pain, but I feel bad for her because she saw Scott kissing another girl and started to cry. How is California? I miss you. I'm thinking of getting another bikini at this store here called If the Suit Fits. Stacey already got another one, of course.

Love,
Mary Anne

P.S. Destroy this card in California!!

Dawn Schafer
88 Palm Blvd.
Palo City, CA 92800

CHAPTER 10

I'M SORRY. I HAVE A REALLY BAD HEADACHE. WOULD IT BE ALL RIGHT IF I DIDN'T GO TO THE BEACH THIS MORNING?
OH, HONEY, OF COURSE.
JUST TAKE IT EASY.

THANKS FOR STICKING ME WITH ALL THE KIDS AGAIN.
LAST NIGHT YOU DRAGGED ME AROUND TO A BILLION STORES LOOKING FOR A PRESENT FOR SCOTT. THEN WHEN YOU SAW HIM WITH THAT GIRL, YOU PRACTICALLY BLAMED **ME.**
WHEN ALL I'VE BEEN **DOING** IS COVERING FOR YOU!
AND YOU DON'T ACTUALLY HAVE A HEADACHE. YOU'RE JUST MOPING OVER SCOTT.
SO?
WHAT'S THE BIG DEAL? IT'S NOT LIKE YOU WON'T HAVE THAT BOY BABY-SITTER THERE TO HELP. HE SURE DOES **LOVE** SHOWING UP WHEN I'M NOT AROUND.
THAT'S -- THAT'S NOT THE POINT.
WHAT POINT?
HOW YOU'VE MADE ME DO **ALL** THE WORK SO FAR! **WE'RE** GETTING PAID TO TAKE CARE OF THE PIKES, NOBODY ELSE.
AND I **HAVE** BEEN!

UM...STACEY?

CAN I STAY WITH YOU THIS MORNING?
I GUESS, BUT I'M NOT FEELING VERY WELL.

DO YOU FEEL LIKE TAKING A WALK? OR ARE YOU TOO SICK?
A WALK MIGHT BE NICE.

...UM, AS LONG AS IT'S SOMEWHERE QUIET.
FOR MY HEADACHE.

OH, I KNOW A REALLY GOOD PLACE. COME ON.

THIS IS THE BAY SIDE OF SEA CITY.
WAIT, IS SEA CITY ON AN ISLAND?
NOPE, JUST A LITTLE PIECE OF LAND THAT CURLS INTO THE OCEAN LIKE A DOG'S TAIL.
THAT'S A NICE WAY TO DESCRIBE IT.
SEE? YOU CAN SEE LAND ACROSS THE WATER. THAT'S THE REST OF NEW JERSEY.

BYRON...
ARE YOU AFRAID OF THE WATER?
WELL...
NOT EXACTLY.
I DON'T LIKE ROUGH WAVES.
AND I DON'T LIKE WHEN I CAN'T SEE THE BOTTOM. ANYTHING COULD BE DOWN THERE.
BUT JORDAN AND ADAM DON'T UNDERSTAND.
THEY THINK I'M A BIG BABY.

IT'S OKAY.
YOU KNOW...
IT'S SMART TO BE A LITTLE AFRAID OF THINGS.
IT IS?

IF YOU AREN'T AFRAID, YOU MIGHT TAKE DANGEROUS CHANCES.
ON THE OTHER HAND, IF YOU'RE **TOO** AFRAID...
THEN YOU'LL PROBABLY MISS OUT ON A LOT OF FUN.

THE BOTTOM'S HIDDEN HERE. HOW DO YOU KNOW IT'S NOT THE EDGE OF A CLIFF?
WELL... I DON'T.
BUT IF IT IS, WE CAN TURN AROUND AND SWIM RIGHT BACK, CAN'T WE?

AS I WALKED WITH BYRON THAT MORNING, ENJOYING THE QUIET OF THE BAY, I FINALLY STARTED TRYING TO UNTANGLE THE KNOT OF FEELINGS DEEP IN MY CHEST.
IT WASN'T LIKE I'D EVER ASKED SCOTT OUT, OR VICE VERSA...
SO I KNEW I COULDN'T REALLY BE MAD AT HIM.
scuttle
I WAS JUST SO EMBARRASSED THAT I'D COMPLETELY MISINTERPRETED WHAT WAS GOING ON BETWEEN US.
AND I DIDN'T THINK I'D BE ABLE TO SPEND ANY MORE TIME AROUND HIM, OR THE GROUP.
EVEN THOUGH IT WASN'T ANYONE'S FAULT...THE HURT WAS A LITTLE TOO FRESH.

THANKFULLY, SCOTT'S SHIFT ENDED JUST AS BYRON AND I GOT TO THE BEACH.

THAT GAVE ME SOME TIME TO CLEAR MY HEAD.

AND IT MADE ME REALIZE...

EVEN THOUGH I'D SPENT ALL THIS TIME AROUND THE KIDS?

I HADN'T REALLY BEEN **WITH** THEM.

AND, TO BE HONEST... I'D BEEN A BAD FRIEND, TOO.

HEY, MARY ANNE.

SORRY I'VE BEEN A COMPLETE JERK.

I SHOULD HAVE PAID MORE ATTENTION TO YOU AND THE KIDS.
AND, UM, NOT LET MY CRUSH GET IN THE WAY OF MY JOB.
AND I SHOULD HAVE LISTENED TO YOU WHEN YOU TRIED TO TELL ME THAT.
I'M REALLY SORRY, MARY ANNE.
APOLOGY ACCEPTED.

Burger Garden
"Where every meal is an adventure!"
3300 Boardwalk • Sea City, NJ

Dear Kristy,

Wednesday

Byron went in the water! (Sort of.) I know what he's afraid of. We'll talk about it at the next BSC meeting. I heard a really funny joke today. I'll tell that at the next meeting, too.

Luv,
Stacey

Kristy Thomas
1210 McLelland Rd.
Stoneybrook, CT 06800

Wednesday

Dear Claudia,

Sadness over! I met a cute guy named Toby. I mean, <u>really</u> cute. He has brown hair, brown eyes, and a few freckles. His clothes are <u>extremely</u> cool.

Luv ya,
Stace

Claudia Kishi
Sky Mountain Resort
Lincoln, NH 03251

CHAPTER 11

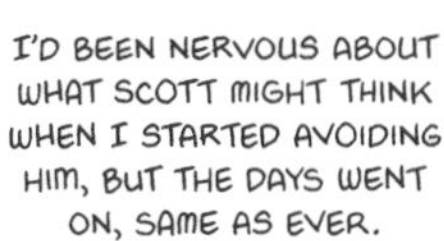

I'D BEEN NERVOUS ABOUT WHAT SCOTT MIGHT THINK WHEN I STARTED AVOIDING HIM, BUT THE DAYS WENT ON, SAME AS EVER.

I PLAYED WITH THE KIDS AND DID MY BEST NOT TO LOOK HIS WAY...

ALTHOUGH SOMETIMES I COULDN'T HELP MYSELF.

AND THEN, SUDDENLY, IT WAS WEDNESDAY.
HMM. YOU KNOW WHAT?

I THINK SOME OF THE KIDS ARE ACTUALLY GETTING BORED OF THE BEACH.
MAYBE WE SHOULD SPLIT UP?

I WOULD HAVE LIKED TO SKIP THE BEACH MYSELF, BUT MARY ANNE WAS WORRIED ABOUT GETTING ANOTHER SUNBURN, SO...OFF WE WENT.

IT WOULDN'T BE TOO BAD, THOUGH. I COULD JUST RELAX, ENJOY THE SEA AIR, AND --
STUPEY-STUPEY-SILLY-BILLY-GOO-GOO!

YOU'RE A STUUUUPEY --
CLAIRE!
WHAT ARE YOU **DOING?**
NOBODY WANTS TO PLAY WITH ME!
THEY'RE ALL IN THE WATER!

THAT'S NO REASON TO CALL ANYBODY NAMES. SAY YOU'RE SORRY, AND THEN GO LIE DOWN ON YOUR TOWEL FOR TEN MINUTES.

SORRY.

UH-OH.
UM, SORRY. CLAIRE WAS TEASING HIM.

NO PROB. KIDS DO THAT. HEY, YOU'RE STACEY, RIGHT?
YEAH. AND YOU'RE ALEX.

YUP. AND THESE ARE ELLIE, JIMMY, KENNY...

AND MY COUSIN TOBY.

HEY! UH. DO YOU KNOW HOW TO MAKE A WITCH'S CASTLE?

WITCH'S CASTLE??

FIRST, WE SIT A LITTLE CLOSE TO THE WATER.
THAT'S BECAUSE WE NEED WET SAND.
PICK SOME UP...
glorp
AND THEN LET IT DRIP THROUGH YOUR FIST, LIKE THIS.
OHHH.
dribble
MERMAID

HA HA! IT'S DRIPPY!!
gloop

HEY, THANKS FOR HANGING OUT WITH US TODAY. I HAD A REALLY GREAT TIME.

ME TOO.

SEE YOU TOMORROW? I PROMISE I'LL TELL ONLY **ONE** LONG BAD JOKE.

YOU CAN HAVE TWO, BUT YOU'VE GOT TO TELL ME MORE ABOUT YOUR BAND.

DEAL.

TOBY WAS THIRTEEN YEARS OLD AND LIVED IN NEW JERSEY.

BYE-BYE, TOBY-SILLY-BILLY-GOO-GOO!

HE WAS THOUGHTFUL, CUTE, AND FUNNY.

SEA CITY,
NEW JERSEY
Wish you
were here!

TUNNEL of LOVE

POSTCARD

Dear Kristy,

Friday

The kids are antsy. It's their last day here. They want to do everything "one last time." But they're also excited about going home. I'll probably see you before you get this card!

Luv,
Stacey

Kristy Thomas
1210 McLelland Rd.
Stoneybrook, CT 06800

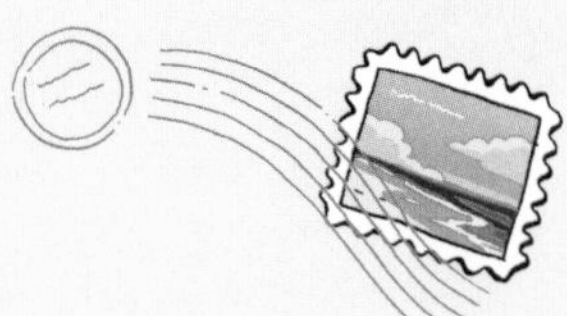

Dear Claudia,

Friday

I'm going out with Toby tonight. For real! We have an evening on the boardwalk planned. I'll tell you all about it when I see you.

Luv ya!
Stace

Claudia Kishi
Sky Mountain Resort
Lincoln, NH 03251

CHAPTER 12

AND THEN, JUST LIKE THAT...
FRIDAY HAD COME.
OUR LAST DAY IN SEA CITY.
I COULDN'T BELIEVE IT WAS ALMOST OVER...
BUT THIS VACATION STILL HAD SOME SURPRISES LEFT UP ITS SLEEVE.
YOU TWO DESERVE ANOTHER NIGHT OFF. WE'LL TAKE OVER AT FIVE O'CLOCK.
OH!
IT'LL BE SO MUCH FUN!
WE CAN CHECK FOR SOUVENIRS AGAIN...EAT SOME FUNNEL CAKE...
OR...

YOU COULD SEE IF ALEX CAN GET TONIGHT OFF, TOO.
WE COULD ALL GO TO THE BOARDWALK OR SOMETHING.

YOU, ME, ALEX, AND TOBY.
T-TOGETHER?

YEAH! LIKE A DOUBLE DATE.
I'M NOT SURE...

YOU KNOW, THIS COULD BE OUR LAST CHANCE.

WE PROBABLY WON'T SEE EITHER OF THEM AFTER THIS TRIP.
THAT'S... THAT'S TRUE.

SO THAT'S SETTLED! GO SEE IF ALEX CAN GET THE NIGHT OFF.
ACK!!

WELL? WELL??

WE'RE MEETING THEM AT HERCULES HOT DOGS AT SIX O'CLOCK.

Our last day:

WALK
RIES
FRENCH FRIES
GIFTS

ULES
DOGS

TOBY! ALEX!
HEY! YOU GUYS LOOK GREAT.

WHO'S READY FOR SOME WORLD-FAMOUS HOT DOGS?
I CAN'T WAIT!
I HEARD THIS PLACE HAS GOOD VEGGIE DOGS.

JUST LIKE WITH THE FLOWERS, JIMMY HAD TO WAIT BEHIND A LONG LINE OF OTHER PROCRASTINATORS TO GET HIS SUIT. BUT, THANK GOODNESS, HE FINISHED JUST IN TIME TO TAKE AMY TO THE DANCE.
THE FIRST THING SHE DID WAS ASK HIM TO GET HER A DRINK, SO HE WENT UP TO GET HER A CUP OF PUNCH...AND WOULDN'T YOU KNOW IT? AFTER ALL THAT, THERE WAS NO PUNCH LINE.
ha
PLEASE TELL ME YOU DON'T KNOW ANY MORE JOKES.
ha ha

HEY... MARY ANNE?

WOULD IT BE OKAY IF WE SPLIT UP AFTER DINNER?
I MEAN, WOULD YOU FEEL OKAY ABOUT BEING ALONE WITH ALEX?

YEAH. YEAH, LET'S DO IT.

T DOGS
TODAY'S
Chili
Dog
SKILL
$

HEY, STACEY?
I GOT YOU SOMETHING.
TO REMEMBER ME BY.
TOBY...
THANK YOU.
TUNNEL of LOVE

sea
City
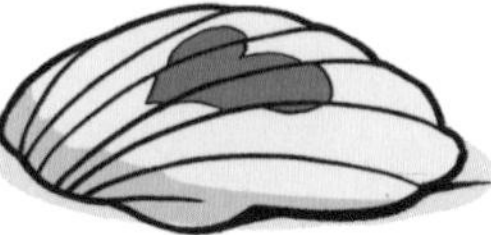

CHAPTER 13
STACEY-SILLY-BILLY-GOO-GOO?
CLAIRE? WHAT ARE YOU DOING?
LOOKING FOR MY SWIMSUIT.
WILL YOU COME TO THE BEACH WITH ME?
SURE, BUT IT'S TOO COLD FOR A SUIT. WHY DON'T YOU GET DRESSED VERY QUIETLY AND I'LL MEET YOU DOWNSTAIRS?

Stacey
+
Toby

BEFORE OUR MAGICAL BEACH VACATION COULD COME TO AN END...

WE STILL HAD ONE THING LEFT TO DO.

HEY, HEY, EVERYBODY!

GUESS WHAT IT'S TIME FOR!

THE CHORE HAT!

NOOOOOOO!

I'VE PUT THE NAMES OF EIGHT CHORES IN THE HAT.

WE HAVE TO LEAVE BY ONE O'CLOCK, SO LET'S ALL DO OUR BEST!

STACEY, MARY ANNE, CAN YOU TWO SUPERVISE THE CHILDREN'S PACKING?

AND TAKE SOME TIME TO PACK UP YOURSELVES, OF COURSE.

I CAN'T BELIEVE WE'RE GOING HOME.
IT FEELS LIKE WE JUST GOT HERE.

BUT WE SURE MADE A LOT OF MEMORIES, DIDN'T WE?
THE KIDS' SUNBURN REMEDIES...
THE LOOK ON ADAM'S FACE WHEN NICKY GOT THE HOLE IN ONE?
THE LOOK ON **YOUR** FACE WHEN YOU WENT TO ASK ALEX ON A DOUBLE DATE!
IT'S ALMOST OVER.

I...DIDN'T TELL YOU ABOUT PART OF MY DATE.
OH??
WE FOUND THIS PLACE WHERE YOU CAN BUY RINGS AND HAVE STUFF ENGRAVED ON THEM.
THEY WERE ONLY A FEW DOLLARS, UM, SO I GOT HIM ONE WITH MY INITIALS...
agw
AND HE GOT ME ONE WITH HIS. TO REMEMBER EACH OTHER BY.
MARY ANNE!!
I JUST HAVE TO MAKE SURE DAD DOESN'T SEE IT. HE'D GO BALLISTIC.
ha
ha

THE KIDS FINISHED UP THEIR CHORES EARLY ENOUGH THAT WE ALL HAD TIME FOR ONE LAST SWIM AT THE BEACH.

I TRIED TO CAPTURE IT ALL IN MY MEMORY. THE SALTY AIR, THE WARM SAND, THE SUN --

HEY! SIT WITH US.

SORRY, WE'RE JUST OUT FOR A QUICK WALK. WE HAVE TO GET BACK...

BUT WE WANTED TO SAY GOOD-BYE.

OH NO. I HATE GOOD-BYES.

PROMISE YOU'LL WRITE?
YEAH.
I'LL EVEN SEND SOME REALLY LONG BAD JOKES.
WILL YOU REMEMBER ME?
ALWAYS.

IFEGUARD+L
GUARD+

BARF-
MOBILE

CHAPTER 14

I'M HOME!
STACEY!!
HOW **ARE** YOU!
DID YOU HAVE FUN?
hug!!
DID YOU TAKE YOUR INSULIN EVERY DAY? DID YOU WEAR SUNBLOCK? DID YOU --
I HAD A GREAT TIME, I KEPT TO MY DIET AND INSULIN...
AND I DIDN'T GET SICK EVEN ONCE.

I'm SO **PROUD** OF YOU.

I KNOW WE'VE BEEN TWO BIG WORRYWARTS THROUGH ALL THIS, BUT, STACEY...YOU'VE BEEN VERY RESPONSIBLE.

WE'LL TRY TO BE BETTER ABOUT TRUSTING YOU MORE.

I CAN'T BELIEVE I'M TALKING TO YOU, IT FEELS LIKE IT'S BEEN YEARS!

HOW ARE YOU? HOW WAS THE TRIP?

I GOT ALL YOUR POSTCARDS!

OH! I'M REALLY SORRY ABOUT SCOTT.

ha ha

HOW ARE **YOU?**

GREAT! I THINK THE MOUNTAIN AIR WAS REALLY GOOD FOR MIMI.
AND THERE WERE ARTS AND CRAFTS THERE, AND I GOT TO THROW A POT.
YOU **WHAT?** WHY?
HA HA! THAT'S WHAT THEY CALL IT WHEN YOU MAKE A POT. ON A POTTER'S WHEEL. YOU **THROW** IT.
OH.
MOM AND DAD REALLY LIKED IT. THEY SAID MAYBE I COULD TAKE A CLASS HERE WHEN SCHOOL STARTS!
THAT'S GREAT! DID YOU MEET ANY INTERESTING GUYS?
OH, YOU KNOOOOW.
I MET THIS REAL CHARMER NAMED SKIP. PERFECT HAIR, GORGEOUS EYES...
AND??
THREE YEARS OLD...
BOOOOO.
BUT WHAT ABOUT **YOU?!**
WHAT HAPPENED WITH SCOTT? AND **TOBY??**
WELL...

WE TALKED FOR HOURS. ABOUT OUR VACATIONS, ABOUT EVERYTHING I'D NOTICED ABOUT THE PIKE KIDS...
AND ABOUT --
YOU KISSED? YOUR FIRST KISS?!!
YOU DIDN'T SAY ANYTHING ABOUT THAT! DETAILS! DETAILS!!!
I COULDN'T BELIEVE THAT OUR BEACH TRIP HAD COME AND GONE SO QUICKLY.
IN JUST A FEW WEEKS, WE'D BE BACK AT SCHOOL...
NEW YORK CITY
STARTING EIGHTH GRADE, AND GETTING INTO ALL SORTS OF NEW ADVENTURES.

BUT FOR NOW...
I HAD A BEAR...
A SHELL...

AND FOND MEMORIES THAT I KNEW I'D HOLD ON TO FOREVER.

Burger Garden
ADMIT ONE

MINI

ANN M. MARTIN'S The Baby-sitters Club is one of the most popular series in the history of publishing — with more than 176 million books in print worldwide — and inspired a generation of young readers. Her novels include *Belle Teal, A Corner of the Universe* (a Newbery Honor book), *Here Today, A Dog's Life,* and *On Christmas Eve,* as well as the much-loved collaborations, *P.S. Longer Letter Later* and *Snail Mail No More,* with Paula Danziger, and *The Doll People* and *The Meanest Doll in the World,* written with Laura Godwin and illustrated by Brian Selznick. She lives in upstate New York.

GALE GALLIGAN is the creator of *New York Times* bestselling graphic novel adaptations of *Dawn and the Impossible Three* and *Kristy's Big Day* by Ann M. Martin. When Gale isn't making comics, she enjoys knitting, reading, and spending time with her adorable pet rabbits. She lives in Pleasantville, New York. Visit her online at galesaur.com.

DON'T MISS THE OTHER BABY-SITTERS CLUB GRAPHIC NOVELS!

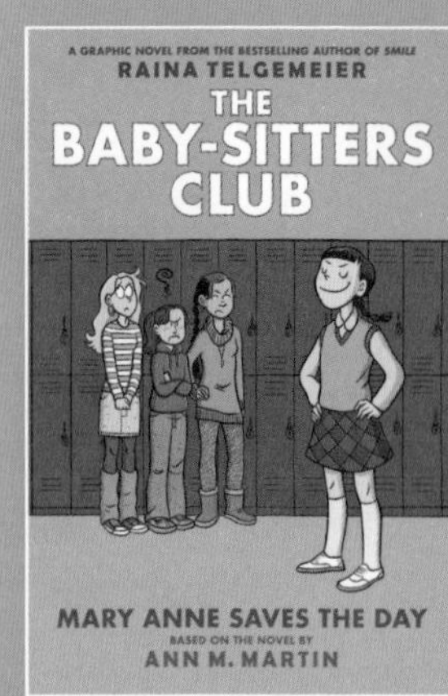